The Ghost on the Hill

The Ghost on the Hill

by Grace Maccarone

illustrated by Kelly Oechsli
Cover art by Carol Newsom

A
LITTLE APPLE
PAPERBACK

SCHOLASTIC INC.

New York   Toronto   London   Auckland   Sydney

ISBN 0-590-42978-7

Copyright © 1990 by Grace Maccarone
All rights reserved. Published by Scholastic Inc.

APPLE PAPERBACKS is a registered trademark of Scholastic Inc.

12 11 10 9 8 7 6 5 4 3 2 1   0 1 2 3 4 5/9

Printed in the U.S.A.   42

First Scholastic Printing, September 1990

To Eva and Diane

*And thanks to Terry Ruyter and her terrific class—
Brandy, Jesse, Jackie, Samantha, Orit, Jacob,
Vanessa, Abby, Paris, Benjamin, Lisa, Pamela,
Ashley, Matthew, Joshua, Baht, and Rachel.*

The Ghost on the Hill

Prologue

WHAT WAS THAT sound?

A black braid struck Lightfoot's cheek as he quickly turned his head to glimpse the white tail of a fleeting deer. No danger.

Nine winters had passed in Lightfoot's life. This morning he awoke a boy. Tonight he would return a Wannatuck brave — or not return at all.

The priest, the Wisest One, had left him at Weeping Brook. Now Lightfoot was alone in the Dark Forest in search of the Spirit of the Hill.

If the Spirit gave his blessing, they would dance together. If the Spirit did not give his blessing, Lightfoot would be banished from the tribe. His mother and sisters would mourn him. His father and brothers would forget him.

Lightfoot had to keep his thoughts pure or the evil spirits of the forest would find him first and make him their slave.

The Wisest One waited and watched.

The air grew cool as Lightfoot walked toward his fate. There were many dangers in the Dark Forest.

Lightfoot heard the rustling of leaves. Was it a bear? Or a wolf? The evil spirits of the forest? The angry spirit of a banished tribesman? He did not know.

He longed for the safety of the longhouse and his mother's arms. Then he was ashamed.

Lightfoot continued to walk to the top of the hill. He moved with the steps of a deer, the ears of a fox, and the eyes of an owl.

He prayed he would not run away at the sight of the Great Spirit. He hoped the Spirit of the Hill was not very big or very ugly.

Lightfoot watched the sun set as he reached the top of the hill. His fox ears heard a startling sound behind him. As he turned, he saw the giant figure of the Spirit. Lightfoot froze in his place. The Great Spirit was equally as still.

Lightfoot's legs felt weak as he began the dance his father taught him. The Spirit began the same slow dance.

Now I am a man! Lightfoot was proud and joyful. He danced faster and faster and faster and faster until the sun disappeared and the Great Spirit disappeared with it.

Lightfoot was saying a prayer of thanks when the priest, the Wisest One, came to take him back to the tribe. And the celebration began.

Another winter passed. Then spring, when an English fur trader brought a deadly disease to the Wannatuck tribe. Only one young brave lived to tell the tales of his people.

Many years passed. The land had become a state park where students went to learn about animals and trees and the Wannatuck who had lived and died there.

No one had danced with the Great Spirit for a long, long time.

Chapter One

ADAM JOHNSON, DAYDREAMER and third-grade ghosthunter, carefully looked to his left, then to his right. The coast is clear, he thought. He crossed the street. He was safe. There was not a ghost — nor a car — in sight.

But Adam had a strange feeling that something was watching him. And that something wasn't animal, vegetable, or mineral. That something was a ghost!

Ghosts had taken over Elmwood. They were moving into people's houses, eating all their food, and taking all the seats in the movie house.

Only one person could save the town. One smart and fearless third-grader. The townspeople shouted his name: "Adam! Adam! Adam!"

Chuck Webber's voice ended Adam's daydream. "Knock-knock."

Chuck had just bought a whole book of knock-knock jokes.

Adam played along.

"Who's there?" Adam said.

"Arch."

"Arch who?"

"Bless you!"

After he told a joke, Chuck's green eyes seemed to disappear into his rosy round cheeks.

Chuck had a style all his own. He wore his baseball cap with the visor shading the back of his neck. And he always wore his sweatshirts, which usu-

ally hugged his round tummy, inside-out.

"Are you packed for tomorrow?" Chuck asked.

Chuck and Adam and the rest of the third grade were going on a class trip to State Forest.

"My mom got everything ready over the weekend," Adam said. "And you?"

"My mom did it last night," Chuck said.

Adam was excited. He would be away from his parents. But he would be away from his stuffed monkey, Zeppo, too. Adam wouldn't dare let the other kids know about Zeppo.

"No pesky brother for three whole days," Adam said.

"And no dumb sisters for three whole days," said Chuck.

"I'm going to stay up all night," said Adam.

"Both nights!" said Chuck.

The boys walked down the wooded path that led to the old Blackwell mansion. The four third-grade classes of Elmwood Elementary were in that spooky old house because the school's main building was too crowded.

As Adam and Chuck walked closer to the grassy play yard, they saw a group of third-graders huddled around Debbie Clark.

"What's up?" Adam asked.

"It's my rock collection," Debbie said. "My aunt bought it for me at a museum."

"Wow!" said Adam. "Let me see."

Debbie's collection had rocks from all around the country. All the rocks were labeled. There was hematite from Minnesota, calcite from New Mexico, malachite from Arizona, and rhodo-chrosite from New Jersey. Adam's favorite was a shiny piece of obsidian that came from Colorado.

"That's not such a big deal," said Joey Baker. Joey had a small, thin voice that matched his small, thin body. "I found a diamond this big in our back-yard." Joey cupped his hands to make a circle the size of a Ping-Pong ball.

"No way," said Chuck.

"Prove it," said Jeff Arnold.

"Yeah, prove it," said Chuck.

"I lost it," Joey said.

Chapter Two

AFTER SHOW-AND-TELL, some of the boys and girls in Mr. Jenkins's class gave their reports on American Indians.

Chuck reported on Indian food.

Kim reported on Indian clothing.

Dan reported on Indian sports.

It was late in the afternoon. Norma Hamburger was the last to give her report for the day.

Norma walked to the front of the room. She pushed her glasses up to the bridge of her nose. Then she began to read.

"Indians had two names. One was a special name that was not often used. They believed that this special name might wear out if it was used too often. An Indian's best friends might not even know this name.

"The other name was like a nickname. This name told something about the person.

"An Indian named Many Goats owned many goats. An Indian named The Weaver was the best weaver in her tribe.

"Red Cloud was a great chief. He was born on a night when a meteor left a trail of red clouds. The clouds looked red. So his mother named him Red Cloud."

While Norma read, Adam watched the clock. She finished just one minute before the dismissal bell would ring.

And Mr. Jenkins hadn't given any homework.

"That was great, Norma," Mr. Jenkins said. "And it gives me an idea for a homework assignment."

"Awwwwww . . ."

A low murmur spread through the classroom. No one wanted homework before the class trip. Not even Norma Hamburger. And she usually liked homework.

Mr. Jenkins ignored the murmur and continued. "I want each of you to think of an Indian name for yourself.

The name could tell something about who you are or what you are like. It could tell about something you have or something you did. It could tell about something that happened when you were born."

It wasn't such a bad homework assignment after all. Most of the kids in the class cheered up.

But not Joey.

Chapter Three

ON THE MORNING of the class trip, Adam woke up before dawn.

At six o'clock in the morning Adam's mother, with both hands on the wheel, her back stiff, and her eyes on the road, was driving Adam to school.

"Why do we have to pick up Joey?" Adam asked.

"With a new baby and twelve other kids, Mrs. Baker needs all the help she can get," said Mrs. Johnson.

"Joey's weird," said Adam. "He lies all the time."

16

Adam's mother didn't say anything as she stopped for a red light. Adam pretended that there were two ghosts in the backseat. He slouched down in his seat, then quickly popped up and turned around. He pointed his finger. "Pshew-pshew-pshew! Gotcha!"

"Sit in your seat, Adam," his mother said. Adam's mother didn't like him to fidget while she was driving.

It was hard for Adam to be still. He tried to think of an Indian name for himself. Maybe he could come up with a cool name like Red Cloud. Maybe his mother could help.

"What was it like on the night I was born?" Adam asked.

"It was cold," said his mother. "Very cold."

"What did you see in the sky? Meteor showers? A comet? A red sunset?"

"I didn't see the sky," his mother

said. "I was in a hospital room. I saw a bed, a chair, and a fetal monitor."

His mother wasn't helping at all. Who wanted to be named Fetal Monitor? Adam didn't even know what that was.

"What did I look like?" Adam asked.

"Well, you were screaming. And you were kind of purple. And you were covered with white stuff. Your hair was wet, and you had dark curls that stuck to your head. You were so cute."

Cute Boy? No way. Adam didn't think his mother's description sounded so cute anyway.

Screaming Boy? Not bad.

Chapter Four

JOEY'S HOUSE HAD its own bicycle rack
and a row of seven bicycles: a pink
twenty-inch bike with training wheels,
a well-worn green twenty-incher without training wheels, a black BMX, a
brand-new three-speed touring bike,
a snappy blue ten-speed racing bike, a
red tricycle with a white basket, and a
yellow plastic trike with Big Bird's face
in the middle of the handlebars.

Mrs. Johnson pulled into the drive-
way, and Adam got out of the car. He
was about to ring the doorbell when

a girl wearing a sling filled with news-papers walked out the door.

"Joey's room is on the top of the staircase. First one on the right," she said.

Adam knew that girl. Her name was Diane, and she was the county spelling champ.

In the hallway, Adam was stopped in his tracks by a giggling, bare-bottomed toddler. Not far behind, a large, muscular, teenaged boy waved a disposable diaper.

"I'm gonna get you." The teenager was smiling.

Adam recognized him from the local newspaper. He was the star quarterback of the junior high school football team.

The baby darted around the sofa, the coffee table, and two well-worn armchairs before the teenager scooped her up like a giant football.

"Gotcha!" he said. But he wasn't in time. Adam saw the puddle and giggled as he skipped up the steps.

"Maaaaaaa!" Joey shouted. Half of his head was under a bed. "Where's my flashlight? I can't find my flashlight and Adam will be here any minute."

"I'm here already," Adam said. He saw a half-empty duffel bag and a list in Joey's hand.

"You don't have to rush," Adam said. "We're still early."

Just then, Joey's mother came to the door. She was carrying Joey's newest brother. His nose was flat and his eyes were mostly closed. He had a tiny mouth and chin and giant cheeks that looked as if they were stuffed with cotton.

"You get some breakfast, and I'll finish the packing," she said.

Adam and Joey left the room.

"One thing this family didn't need was another baby," Joey muttered.

"You sure have a lot of kids in your family," Adam said.

"This isn't my family," Joey said. "I'm just staying here until my real parents get back." Joey lowered his voice to a whisper. "Don't tell anyone, but my parents are spies. They're on a very important mission for the government."

One time Joey said his father was a four-star general and his mother was an astronaut. Another time Joey told Adam his parents were scientists. Everyone in Mr. Jenkins's class knew that Joey lied a lot. No one could figure out why.

Chapter Five

By the time Adam and Joey got on the school bus, most of the seats were taken. Adam looked around for a place to sit. Chuck was already sitting next to Dan. Sam was sitting next to Keith. Debbie was sitting next to Norma, and Matty was sitting next to Haseeb.

Jeff Arnold was spread across two seats. Jeff was the class bully. Adam wouldn't have wanted to sit next to him anyway.

Adam was stuck sitting next to Joey Baker for the whole trip. Luckily,

24

there were two seats in front of Adam's buddies, Chuck and Dan.

"Knock-knock," said Chuck.

"Who's there?" said Dan.

"Little old lady."

"Little old lady who?" said Dan.

Chuck laughed. "I didn't know you could yodel."

"I have a good Indian name for you," said Dan. "Laughing Boy."

"I have a better one," said Jeff. "Meathead."

Chuck laughed. "Call me whatever you want. Just don't call me late for supper!"

"Let's think of a name for Dan," said Adam. "Uhhh . . . what about Big Boy?"

"That's the name of a sandwich," Chuck said.

"I think Dan should be Little Bear," said Norma Hamburger. "Little Bear sounds like a real Indian name."

Everyone agreed that Little Bear would be a good name for Dan, who was as big and strong as a bear — a little bear, that is.

The third-graders spent most of the bus ride thinking of names for themselves. Debbie Clark was going to be Girl Who Loves Science. Kim decided upon Crystal Brook and Liz picked Dancing Flower.

"Norma can be Four Eyes," said Jeff.

"I don't want to be Four Eyes," said Norma.

"Norma can be Smart Girl," said Adam.

But Norma didn't want to be Smart Girl either. She wanted a pretty name — like Dancing Flower or Crystal Brook.

"What do you think of White Cloud?" Norma asked Debbie.

"Pew," said Debbie. "That's the name of a toilet paper."

Norma giggled. "That's right. I forgot."

Then she had an idea. More than anything, Norma liked to read. She would name herself after a book. Norma started to think of her favorite books.

Wizard of Oz? No.

Winnie the Pooh? No.

Veronica the Show-off? No way!

The Cat Who Went to Heaven? No.

Blue Willow? Perfect! Norma would name herself Blue Willow!

"What about me?" asked Joey.

But no one could think of a name for Joey except for mean Jeff Arnold. Joey could be "Boy Who Speaks with Forked Tongue," said Jeff.

"What does that mean?" Dan asked Chuck.

Chuck whispered a reply in Dan's ear.

"It means Boy Who Lies a Lot," Jeff said out loud.

Joey was so ashamed. More than anything, he wanted to think of a really special name for himself.

The entrance to State Forest had two stone columns. Most of the third-graders did not notice them. It had been a smelly, bumpy ride, and most of the girls and boys felt sick.

The bus pulled up to Huckapoo Lodge. The long, low, wooden brown building looked about a hundred years old. The girls would stay there.

The bus continued down a road that bordered a large lake.

"Tomorrow we go rowing," said Mr. Jenkins.

"Cool," said Chuck.

"Yeah," said Adam. "My father takes me rowing in the park all the time."

"I went rowing last year at camp," said Dan.

Joey was angry. Four older brothers, two older sisters, two parents, and no one had ever thought to take him rowing. But he did not want to admit it. Everyone would think he was a nerd.

"I've been rowing a million times," he said.

But he wished he had not said it. Tomorrow they would find out that he couldn't row a boat. And they would tease him.

Just then, the bus pulled up to the side of another old, low, wooden building.

"This makes the girls' bunk look like a luxury hotel," said Chuck.

The inside of the flat building smelled of old smoke and damp wood.

"Home, sweet home," said Dan as he threw his duffel bag across a cot.

Adam threw his bag on the cot next to Dan's. "Let the fun begin," he said.

Chapter Six

LUNCH WAS PINK and white meat between two slices of white bread smeared with butter. Things had to get better after that.

And they did.

The third-graders were able to choose from different workshops. Norma Hamburger chose a workshop called Art in Nature. Debbie Clark went on the Geology Trail to find new rocks and minerals for her collection. Kim and Liz went to Home Life in Colonial Days.

Adam, Chuck, Joey, and Dan went to Indian Lore. They looked at a real tomahawk. And they held real Indian arrowheads in their hands.

Their workshop leader was a tall, thin man with straight black hair and smiling brown eyes.

"My name is Dennis Ten Foot Bridge," he said. "And I am a Wannatuck. I am the only living descendant of the tribe that lived here over a hundred years ago."

Wow! thought Joey. Debbie can keep her old rocks. This is definitely the best workshop of all.

"What does your name mean?" Joey asked. He imagined that Dennis Ten Foot Bridge had done something very brave. Maybe he dived off a ten foot bridge to rescue a drowning child.

Dennis Ten Foot Bridge just shrugged. "I don't know," he said. "It was my father's name. And my grand-father's name, too.

"How old are you?" Dennis Ten Foot Bridge asked Joey.

"Nine," Joey said proudly. His birthday had been just last week.

"Well, at your age, you would be ready to become a man. When a boy reached his ninth birthday, he went on a vision quest. The day before, he would eat nothing but a special por-ridge. He would pray to the Great Spirit. His family would also pray. Then in the late afternoon, the boy would set out on his journey.

"The priest would take him to the Weeping Brook. After that, the boy would be on his own. He had to keep his thoughts pure or the evil spirits of the forest would find him first and make him their slave. The boy would walk through the Dark Forest until the Great Spirit would show himself and dance."

Joey was glad he wasn't a Wannatuck. He didn't feel ready to be a man. Not yet.

"Did you have to go on a vision quest?" Chuck asked Dennis Ten Foot Bridge.

"Not quite," Dennis said. "Though I have gone camping here in the Dark Forest. It's called the Dark Forest because the trees are so dense in some places that the sun can't shine through. . . . Anyway, I study the old ways. But I don't really practice them."

"Do you think there are real spirits around here?" Adam asked. If there were, Adam wanted to find them.

Dennis Ten Foot Bridge just raised his eyebrows.

Chapter Seven

IF HE HAD been a more popular kid, someone would have noticed he was gone. But Joey was not a popular kid. It had been easy for him to slip out of the mess hall at supper time.

A path lead directly from the mess hall to the lake. But Joey could not take it. He could not risk being seen by anyone. He did not want anyone to stop him.

The mess hall smells of barbecue sauce and garbage soon gave way to the fresh smell of pine. Joey walked

through the forest among tall trees that blocked out the light from the setting sun. He waded through ferns and vines that reached chest-high, whipping his arms and tangling around his calves. And he tripped over logs and stones.

The empty lake looked even larger than Joey had expected. A long row of boats were set on their sides like a chorus line of giant fish shining silvery in the setting sun.

Joey stumbled over a tree stump in his path. His heart beat faster, though his legs moved slower.

Joey pulled one of the rowboats off its side. It landed on the dock with a thump. Joey looked around to see if the noise attracted anyone.

It didn't. Joey was alone.

He pushed the boat so that only the tip remained on the dock. His legs felt rubbery from nervousness. He climbed in, cautious as a cat. But the boat rocked, startling him, and Joey fell.

"Oars!" he said aloud to himself. He climbed out and took two oars from a pile. He lay them in the boat and climbed back in. This time the rocking did not startle him.

Joey pushed off with the oars. The boat bobbed in the water, still hugging the dock. Joey placed the oars in the two hooks on the side of the boat and sat down on the middle bench. He practiced moving the oars in the air, then dipped them in the water. He did not know if he should push out or pull in, so he tried both ways.

Joey pushed out. Nothing happened. Then he pulled in. He was moving! Joey did it again.

Joey put one oar in the water and pushed. The boat curved. Then he pulled. The boat curved the other way.

Joey aimed for a buoy. His path

was not straight. But at least he got there. As he continued to row, Joey's strokes were more even, and the boat moved in a straighter path.

Joey picked the oars out of the water and let himself drift. He felt happy. He could row a boat just as well as the other boys. No one would laugh at him now.

As Joey drifted toward the shore, a family of ducks — a mother, a father, and thirteen ducklings — passed by. The ducklings swam in a straight row. Each seemed to know exactly where he or she belonged. Not one fell back. Not one tried to move ahead.

Joey watched the ducks and wondered what his own family was doing.

The sun hung low in the sky. In the early evening shadows, the lake was shiny gray. Joey looked toward the sun. The trees were black shadows against a glowing gray-white sky. A gentle breeze blew as the sun dropped.

Joey turned toward the hill. A fluffy white cloud drifted toward the top. The cloud reflected the golden glow of the sun. And the sky grew darker . . . and darker . . . and darker. . . .

The night animals began to stir.

"Whooo . . . whooo . . . whooo. . . ."

Joey did not believe what he saw. There was a huge figure on the top of the hill. The figure stood as still as a statue. Joey blinked to clear his eyes, then looked again. It was still there.

A ghost!

The figure hovered in the sky. It stood up straight — taller than the tallest tree. And then it was gone.

Chapter Eight

THE SUN HAD set. A big round moon lit the sky. The lake was as smooth and shiny and black as Debbie's obsidian.

Joey rowed back to shore as quickly as he could. His arms were tired after an hour of rowing, but fear made him stronger.

Once again Joey had to make his way through the Dark Forest. He could see very little outside the small circle lit by his flashlight. So he was alert to every sensation: the fresh smell of green leaves and pine needles, the sting and itch of insects, the chattering of birds and crickets.

Dry twigs crunched beneath his feet as he walked among animals that did not sleep at night: rats, bats, raccoons, and owls. Mr. Jenkins had taught the class about them earlier that year.

Joey walked cautiously. He could hear the sound of paws scurrying away in the rustling leaves. He knew he frightened the animals. But they frightened him, too. He was bigger. But they had sharp teeth and claws. They could see better at night than he could. They knew the secrets of the forest. They were home. He was not.

"Whooo . . . whooo . . . whooo. . . ."

Joey looked up and saw an owl perched in a tree. The owl ignored Joey. It swooped down without a sound, so fast that Joey could not follow it with his flashlight.

When he found it again, the owl held a large mouse in its mouth. In the next moment, the mouse was gone. The owl, calm and still, stared way out ahead into the woods, to a point way beyond Joey's own field of vision.

Joey saw his cabin and ran, slipping on dried leaves and pine needles, tripping over rocks and fallen branches. When he reached the door, he quietly turned the knob and opened the door just wide enough to squeeze himself in.

"I saw a ghost!"

The other boys stopped what they were doing and turned toward him. No one moved except for Jeff Arnold. He walked over to Joey until he loomed over the smaller boy's head.

"Look who's here," Jeff said. "It's the Boy Who Speaks with Forked Tongue. It's Joey Baker, the crybaby liar."

Joey's voice became thin and weak. "It's true," he said. "I did see a ghost."

He looked at the other boys — Dan, Adam, Chuck, Steve, Sam. Not one of them would stand up for him.

And how could he blame them?

Joey fixed his eyes on the wooden slats of the floor. He couldn't see the other boys, but he knew they were staring as he walked toward his cot and climbed into his sleeping bag.

He lay as still as he could. He didn't dare move — not even to change his clothes, not even to take off his shoes. Joey listened to the other boys talk and laugh until Mr. Jenkins came in to shut the lights and tell them to go to sleep. Then Joey heard the other boys talk and laugh some more. He listened until the talk became softer and the laughter became weaker, and one by one, they fell asleep. Joey was the last.

The next morning, Joey felt miserable. His restless night left him very tired. From inside his sleeping bag, Joey could hear Jeff Arnold making fun of him.

Joey waited until everyone was dressed and off to breakfast before he finally poked his head out of his sleeping bag. He was surprised that Adam was still there.

"So, where did you see the ghost?" Adam asked.

Chapter Nine

ADAM AND JOEY agreed to go after the ghost together. But they had to wait until after breakfast, rowing, lunch, and Wildlife Ecology.

They decided to sneak out during dinner. It had worked for Joey once before. It would probably work again.

"Ready for dinner?" Chuck asked Adam.

"Not yet." Adam pretended to be reading a book. "I want to finish this chapter."

"I'll wait."

"Uh, don't wait," Adam said. "After I finish this chapter, I have to do something else."

Chuck guessed something was up. He would have stayed around to find out about it, but hunger won out over curiosity.

"That was a close call," Joey said after Chuck left the room.

"Yeah," said Adam. "Let's get going."

Adam and Joey decided to go out the back door. They thought they'd have less of a chance of being seen. But they were wrong.

"Hi, boys!" said Mr. Jenkins. "Do you mind if I walk with you to the mess hall?"

Adam and Joey knew they wouldn't be able to get away now.

"I watched you rowing this morning," Mr. Jenkins said to Joey. "You were doing very nicely. You must have done it before."

When they reached the mess hall, Mr. Jenkins left the boys and joined the other teachers at their table.

"He knows I went rowing last night!" Joey said in a panic. "And he knows we're trying to go off on our own tonight!"

"Calm down," said Adam. "If he did, he would have gotten mad and tried to stop us."

"He did stop us!" Joey said.

"No, he didn't," said Adam. "We'll sneak out somehow."

But just then, Chuck and Dan came by. Joey had to think fast.

"I have to get something from my duffel bag," he said.

Adam knew he would not be able to get away as easily.

When the other boys weren't look-

ing, he mouthed out two words to Joey: "I'm trapped!"

Joey was afraid to go back to the lake alone. So he returned to the bunk as he told the others he would.

The evening was cool. Joey took out his duffel bag to get another sweat-shirt. Feeling around along the bottom of the bag, he touched something small and soft. It was Jennie's Ernie doll! Joey wondered how it got in there.

Joey felt around some more and found something smooth and hard. It was his brother Mark's Swiss army knife!

Joey turned the duffel bag upside

down over his cot. It was full of surprises: Matt's football jersey, three of Cathy's favorite chocolate chip cookies, Ellen's pocket camera, Craig's Mickey Mouse compass, and Ted's favorite T-shirt — the one he got from the Ferrara Concrete Company.

Joey found candy and gum and a book — something from each of his brothers and sisters. There was even a picture of Baby Ben, which someone had put in for him.

And then he found the letter. "I miss you. Hugs and kisses, Mom."

Joey gave Ernie a squeeze. He didn't feel afraid anymore. He stuffed his duffel bag with all his presents. Some might be useful. Some might be lucky. And some would just be nice to have around.

Then off he went — in search of the ghost.

Chapter Ten

THE NIGHT CREATURES that lived in the Dark Forest had begun to stir. The bats and rats. The raccoons. The owls.

Joey's nose and fingertips were cold. But he walked on. He walked in the direction of the ghost he had seen the night before.

"Whooo...whooo...whooo...."

Joey looked up and saw an owl. The owl looked back at him. Joey studied its eyes. They looked angry. But why would they be angry with him?

"Whooo...whooo...whooo...."

Joey looked up. The owl was circling him.

Joey walked on, but the owl followed. Not for a moment did it let the boy out of its sight.

Joey thought about his mother. He thought about how she'd miss him if he never came back, and tears came to his eyes.

As the sun set, Joey entered a clearing. He looked up, but the sun burned his eyes. He turned away.

A gentle breeze blew, and a fluffy white cloud drifted toward the top of the mountain. The cloud reflected the golden glow of the sun. And the sky grew darker . . . and darker . . . and darker. . . .

The night animals chirped and howled and hooted all around him.

"Whooo . . . whooo . . . whooo. . . ."

And when he looked up, he saw

it again. The giant ghost at the top of the hill.

The old, fibbing, scaredy-cat Joey would have run away. But this was a new Joey. And the new Joey would not run.

Joey planted his feet firmly on the ground and placed his hand on his hips.

The ghost did the same.

Joey promised himself that he would not be scared off. He waited bravely for the ghost to make a move. But the ghost did not. The ghost stood tall and still. Both boy and ghost were frozen in a silent standoff until . . .

"Whooo . . . whooo . . . whooo. . . ."

Joey looked over his shoulder. The owl was still there. It swooped toward him. Joey ducked just in time.

When he looked back at the giant ghost, it was gone.

And then it was pitch-dark.

Chapter Eleven

ADAM WAS WAITING for Joey outside the cabin.

"So what happened? Did you see anything? Did you see it again?"

But Joey didn't have to answer. Adam could tell by looking at Joey's face. His skin was pale. His eyes were wide. His lips were dry.

"What did it do? Did it fly at you? Did it screech or howl?"

Joey shook his head. "It was *huge*. It seemed to grow right in front of my eyes."

"Tomorrow, we're all going," Adam said. "Dan and Chuck and you and me."

"I thought they didn't believe me," Joey said.

"Well, maybe they do and maybe they don't. They want to see for themselves."

Joey didn't want to go again. He had seen the ghost twice and he was afraid of what could happen the next time. But he was too embarrassed to tell Adam he was scared.

"How will we all get away?" Joey asked. "Mr. Jenkins will notice if four boys are missing."

"I know," Adam said. "But I'll think of something. Don't worry."

Joey was worried. But not about getting away. Joey was worried about a ghost.

A real ghost.

*   *   *

That night there wasn't any talking after Mr. Jenkins turned the lights out. Everyone was too tired from staying awake so late the night before.

Joey curled his knees toward his chest and tried to make himself comfortable in his sleeping bag. The sleeping bag had belonged to Mark. Then Matt used it. Now Joey shared it with Diane. She took it to sleepover parties. Joey could feel bits of popcorn on his toes from Diane's last party.

The sleeping bag had pictures from *E.T.* on it. *E.T.* was one of Joey's favorite movies. On some days he would watch it twice. Matt would tease him. "What time is the next showing?" he'd say.

Joey liked the boy in the movie. He didn't have any friends either. Not until E.T. came along. Joey wished that E.T. would visit him.

Joey fell asleep thinking about E.T. and holding Jennie's Ernie in his hand.

Chapter Twelve

"What's an action Socialization Experience?" Adam asked Mr. Jenkins the next morning.

"It's what you'll be doing after breakfast," he said. "See you there at nine."

At breakfast, Joey only picked at his scrambled eggs. He gave his bacon to Chuck, his milk to Dan, and his toast to Adam.

"Maybe we could look for the ghost *after* dinner," said Chuck.

"No," said Joey. "Both times I saw

the ghost as the sun was going down. We'll have to miss dinner — or get there late."

Chuck glared at him. He never missed a meal in his life. And he didn't plan to start now.

"But Mr. Jenkins will notice that we're missing," Chuck said. "We'll get in big trouble. And we'll never get to go on a class trip again for the rest of our lives!"

Chuck was right.

Breakfast ended and the boys still didn't have a getaway plan.

The boys were on their way to their Action Socialization Experience.

"I wish we could go swimming instead of doing this dumb A.S.E.," Chuck said as they passed the lake.

"You don't even know what it is," said Dan. "How can you say that it's dumb?"

"It just sounds dumb," said Chuck.

"It's too cold for swimming," said Adam. "But it would be great to go rowing again."

The lake shone as brightly as the sun.

"Hey, I know those ducks," Joey said. It was the same family of ducks he had seen two nights ago.

Joey counted the ducklings. There were still thirteen. Joey was glad to see that they were all there.

The row of babies started right up front between the mother and father, then formed a trail behind.

The ducks seemed to drift along without any effort at all. Joey drew closer. He walked slowly and carefully. He did not want to frighten them.

From this close, Joey could see their legs and feet kicking rapidly under the surface of the water.

"That's me," said Joey, pointing

his finger. "That family is big — just like mine. And I'm the duck in the middle.

"I just thought of my Indian name. I'll be Middle Duck."

Mr. Jenkins and Dennis Ten Foot Bridge stood in front of a giant rope web that was tied between two trees. A bell hung in the middle of the web.

"What's that for?" Chuck asked.

"You'll see," Dennis said mysteriously. "But first I want you to choose teams. Adam and Kim can start."

Adam picked Dan, Chuck, Debbie, Norma, and Joey.

"Why did you pick Joey?" Chuck whispered to Adam. "He's so bad at sports."

Adam ignored him.

"Okay, everybody ready?" said Dennis Ten Foot Bridge once the teams were picked. "Now every member of your team has to get through a hole without making the bell ring," Dennis went on.

"What?"

"You heard me, Chuck," Dennis said. "And each member of your team must go through a different hole. You can't all go through the big hole on the bottom.

"This activity is about cooperation.

You'll have to pull together — or else
. . ." Dennis shook the rope.

Ting-a-ling-a-ling. Ting-a-ling-a-ling.

"First you and your teammates
must plan who goes in which hole and
how you will get him or her in there.
And then, you'll do it!"

There were a lot of decisions to
make. Who would go through the big
hole on the bottom? It had to be either
Chuck or Dan. They were the largest.

There were some bigger holes
high off the ground. The stronger kids
would have to lift the lighter kids to
get them in there.

The big hole on the bottom wasn't
as big as Chuck had thought. He had
to crawl on his belly to get through it.

Dan went through another big
hole, about a foot off the ground. His
shoulders were a tight squeeze, but he

walked on his hands and feet until he got up to his knees. Chuck and Adam each took a foot and pushed him through.

Debbie went through on her hands wheelbarrow-style with Dan holding her legs.

"You sure look silly walking that way," Chuck said.

"The idea is to cheer your team-mates on — not insult them," Norma said.

"I call 'em as I see 'em," said Chuck.

Now came the hardest part.

The teams were tied. The holes that were left were very small.

The other team was up. Lori Marino thought she could make it through a small hole on the bottom. She got down on her tummy and wiggled.

Chuck was still angry with Lori from last week when she told Mrs. Bovi he stepped on her flowers. He would have told Mrs. Bovi himself if Lori hadn't tattled on him.

"You'll never make it, worm-breath," Chuck said.

Lori pretended not to hear him as she pushed her arms through up to her elbows.

"Keep your head down," Kim shouted. But it was too late.

Ting-a-ling-a-ling. Ting-a-ling-a-ling.

Joey was next. Norma and Debbie lifted him onto Dan's shoulders. Chuck and Adam were ready for him on the other side.

Joey's hands went through the opening until they reached the top of Chuck's shoulders. Joey held his breath as Adam pulled him through.

He made it!

It was the first time Joey had ever felt proud to be small and skinny.

Joey saved the team.

"I vote that we give Joey a new name," Dan said. "From now on, we'll call him Middle Duck Who Slips Like an Eel." Everyone agreed, and Joey felt proud that they'd given him such a good name.

Chapter Thirteen

THEIR AFTERNOON WORKSHOP leader had wavy black hair that reached her waist, round blue eyes, and rosy cheeks. She wore a plaid button-down shirt, tan shorts, thick socks, and hiking boots. Her name was Angela Rinaldi.

"This afternoon, we will learn and practice orienteering." Angela's voice was smooth and calm. "After I show how to use the compass, I will give you a course to follow. You'll find a red flag at the end of each course. Bring it back to me, and I'll know you got to the right place."

"We're in luck," Adam whispered to Dan.

"Yeah," said Dan. "Angela sure is pretty."

"That's not what I'm talking about," Adam said. "Instead of following the directions she gives us, we'll meet at the top of the hill . . . where Joey saw the ghost last night. If someone looks for us, they'll think we made a mistake trying to follow the course. It's perfect! I'll pass it on to Joey and Chuck."

First Angela taught them how to use the compass and judge distances. She had each of them walk a distance of one hundred feet. As they walked, they counted their steps.

Dan counted forty-eight steps. Adam and Chuck counted fifty steps. Debbie counted fifty-one steps. Joey and Norma counted fifty-two steps.

Now they could figure out how many feet they walked.

70

Then Angela separated the third-graders into groups of three or four. Joey, Dan, Norma, and Debbie were in one group. Adam and Chuck were with Lori Marino.

Chuck read the course for his group. "Walk one hundred feet northeast, then two hundred feet south, and then two hundred feet west. I wonder where that goes."

"Well, we don't have time to find out," Adam said. "We've got a ghost to chase."

Lori put her hands on her hips. "Oh, no, you don't. We're going to follow this course or I'm telling."

Adam and Chuck looked at each other. Adam with disappointment; Chuck with relief. He hated to let down his buddy. But he hated missing supper even more.

"I guess we're following the course," Chuck said.

"Let's get going," said Lori. "I want to be the first group to find our flag and get back. One hundred feet northwest is that way." Lori pointed her finger, then started to count her steps.

Chuck and Adam counted their steps behind her.

Then Chuck stopped counting. "Knock-knock."

"Who's there?" Adam said with a sigh.

"Banana," said Chuck.

"Banana who?"

"Knock-knock," Chuck said again.

"Who's there?"

"Banana."

"Banana who?"

"Knock-knock."

"Who's there?"

"Banana."

Adam started to giggle. "Banana who?"

"Knock-knock."

"Who's there?"

"Orange."

"Orange who?"

"Orange you glad I didn't say banana again?"

Adam and Chuck were laughing.

"Now we go two hundred feet south," said Lori.

"South is that way," Adam said.

"Listen! You guys aren't even paying attention. I say it's this way."

"Okay, okay." Adam didn't want to argue.

The three of them walked on with Lori in the lead.

"This doesn't seem right," Chuck whispered to Adam.

"I think we're headed toward the top of the hill where Joey saw the ghost," Adam whispered back.

"The red flag should be around here somewhere," Lori said. "Help me look for it."

They searched and searched. "I think we'd better give up," said Chuck. "It's getting late."

"It's got to be around here somewhere," Lori said. "Keep looking. Chuck, you look in that cave."

"Angela isn't going to put a flag in a cave," Chuck said, but he went in anyway.

As they looked, the sun began to set. A gentle breeze blew, and a fluffy white cloud drifted toward the top of the hill. The cloud reflected the golden glow of the sun. And the sky grew darker . . . and darker . . . and darker. . . .

The night animals began to stir.

"Whooo . . . whooo . . . whooo. . . ."

"This is exactly how Joey described it," Adam said to Chuck. "It's going to happen! It's going to happen soon!"

"What's going to happen?" Lori asked.

74

Just then, Adam heard a familiar voice.

"I thought you guys would never show up." The voice belonged to Joey. Norma, Debbie, and Dan were with him.

"We didn't think we'd show up either," said Chuck. "But here we are."

"What's going on?" Lori asked.

"It's going to happen soon. Isn't it?" Adam said to Joey.

"Yes," Joey whispered. "Very soon."

"What's going to happen?" Lori shouted.

No one had to answer her. Right before their eyes, not one, but seven giant ghosts appeared at the top of the hill.

Chapter Fourteen

"So it's true!" Chuck exclaimed. "Joey's ghost story is true!"

The boys and girls quickly ran into the cave to hide. Just as quickly, the ghosts disappeared.

"Where do you think they've gone?" Lori asked. "Do you think they could be here in this cave — with us?"

"There has to be a scientific explanation for this," Debbie said nervously.

"Then what is it?" said Chuck.

"Let's keep cool, guys," Adam said.

"No sense panicking." But everyone knew that Adam was as frightened as the rest of them.

The only one who seemed calm was Joey. Suddenly, Joey started to walk out of the cave.

"Where are you going?" Chuck asked.

"Hey, come back here!" Adam shouted.

It was no use. Joey ignored them. He kept walking until he was face to face with a ghost!

Joey stood perfectly still. Back in the cave, the others watched and waited.

"He looks as if he's in a trance," Norma said.

Joey mysteriously raised his arms and swayed back and forth.

The ghost did the same.

Joey shook his hands and stamped his feet.

The ghost did the same.

"What's going on?" Dan asked.

"Maybe they're making some kind of pact," said Chuck.

Lori shivered. "Or maybe the ghost has Joey in its power!"

"It looks as if they're dancing," Norma said.

Joey and the ghost jumped up and down and waved their wrists. Together they swirled around and around and around. Then they fell to the ground.

The ghost disappeared.

"Ha, ha, ha!" Joey laughed. "Ha, ha, ha!"

"He's really gone crazy," Lori said.

"We've got to do something!" said Dan.

But nobody had any ideas.

"Ha, ha, ha!" Joey laughed again. "Hey, everyone," he shouted. "Come out here."

But no one would dare step out of the cave. They were all too scared.

Joey ran back to the cave to get the others. When they saw Joey close up, he seemed to be all right. But no one could be sure.

"Those aren't real ghosts," Joey said.

"What do you mean?" Adam asked.

"They're shadows," Joey explained. "When you stand in the right place, you can cast a shadow on that cloud over there. Come on out. It's really neat!"

"I knew there was a scientific reason for this," Debbie said. "That's why the ghost did everything you did."

Debbie was first out of the cave — with Adam and Norma and the others close behind her.

When they got to the right spot, they saw Joey was right. The ghosts were really shadows.

Everyone danced and jumped and hopped. They kicked their legs and waved their arms. And the shadows traced every move.

"Look, it's getting dark," Debbie said. "We'd better all get back to camp."

The ghosthunters waved and the seven ghosts waved back. Then the sky grew dark. One by one the campers followed Lori down the hill — Screaming Boy, Little Bear, Laughing Boy, Blue Willow, Girl Who Loves Science, and Brave Middle Duck Who Slips Like an Eel.

* * *

From another part of the hill, Dennis Ten Foot Bridge watched and smiled. The Great Spirits had not danced for many years. But tonight they danced again.